Goddesses
Coloring Book

Marty Noble

Dover Publications, Inc.
Mineola, New York

NOTE

Goddesses, or female deities, have played a part in many cultures around the world from ancient times to the present day. In this book featuring 30 detailed and ready-to-color illustrations, you will find Isis, the Egyptian goddess of femininity, Eos, the Greek goddess of the dawn, Pachamama, the Incan goddess of the earth, Guan Yin, the Buddhist goddess of compassion, and many more of these divine females, as well as their place in history.

Copyright

Copyright © 2012 by Dover Publications, Inc.

Bibliographical Note

Goddesses Coloring Book is a new work, first published by Dover Publications, Inc., in 2012.

International Standard Book Number

ISBN-13: 978-0-486-48028-2
ISBN-10: 0-486-48028-3

Manufactured in the United States by Courier Corporation
48028308   2015
www.doverpublications.com

Arianrhod, the Celtic moon goddess whose name means "silver wheel," rules over a magical realm called Caer Sidi. She can shapeshift into a large silver owl, and uses this form to observe mortal life. It is said that through her large, owl eyes, she can see into the depths of the human soul.

Celtic mythology's loving protector of horses, donkeys, and mules, **Epona** leads the soul to the afterlife.

The Valkyrie warrior goddess **Freya** represents love, beauty, and fertility, as well as war and death. In Norse mythology, Freya claims the souls of the bravest warriors who died in battle. She is often depicted with two large, blue cats—gifts from the god, Thor.

3

Idunn is the Norse goddess of youth and springtime. As the Keeper of the Golden Apples, Idunn allows each god and goddess to eat one of her apples each day. Doing so keeps them young and immortal.

As the wife of the all-powerful god Odin, Norse goddess **Frigg** is the highest female deity. She represents love, motherhood, marriage, and fertility.

As far back as history can tell us, domestic cats have been highly regarded in Egyptian civilization—and it is the duty of goddess **Bastet** to protect them. Her protection also extends to the owners of cats.

Egyptian goddess **Isis** is considered representative of ideal femininity, and she is patron of all women, mothers, and children. She is said to have spent time among her people, teaching them the skills of agriculture, and reading.

Ma'at is the Egyptian goddess of moral law. She is a judge in the Egyptian underworld, where she evaluates each dead person by placing his or her heart on a scale that determines whether each individual had "followed Ma'at."

Pomona is the Roman goddess of abundance and agriculture. She watches over fruit trees in particular, and cares for those who cultivate them.

Associated with love, beauty, and vineyards, the Roman goddess **Venus** is perfect in every way, having no physical flaws at all. She has the power to transform weapons into objects of peace.

Diana, the Roman hunting goddess, is also associated with the moon, and wild animals. She is considered protector of all things that are free.

Aphrodite is the Greek goddess of love, desire, beauty, and fertility. She has a magic girdle with the power to make any man she looks upon immediately fall in love with her. Her son is the god of love, Cupid.

The Greek goddess of the dawn, Eos rises up into the sky each morning, and breaks through the night with her rays of light. Her siblings are Helios (the sun) and Selene (the moon).

Athena is the Greek goddess of civilized life, war, artisans, and wisdom. She is the favorite daughter of the king of the gods, Zeus. She is considered the most rational, and most benevolent goddess.

The Greek goddess of earth, **Gaia** is said to be the first deity, having been born from chaos. All other gods and goddesses are said to be descended from her union with Uranus (the sky).

Mayan goddess **Ix Chel** is responsible for sending rain to nourish the land, and is the protector of mothers and children. Ix Chel also has a dark side; she brings floods to the land if she is unhappy.

Pachamama is the Incan goddess of the earth. She protects planting and harvesting, and represents fertility. When she is angered, she turns into a dragon and causes earthquakes.

Chalchiuhtlicue is the Aztec goddess of water, and protector of newborn babies, and fishermen. She is the wife of the rain god, Tlaloc.

Although a goddess of love, Sumerian **Inanna** is wandering, and restless. She causes chaos for those who disobey her, and thus is often associated with war or disaster.

The **White Buffalo Woman** of the Native American tribes Lakota and Sioux is considered the mother of life. She taught the first Native Americans their sacred ceremonies, songs, dances, and traditions. She carries with her a sacred pipe, which she gives as a gift to those who wish to remain in communication with the spirit world.

Oshun is the West African goddess of love and fresh water.
She heals the sick and brings both fertility and prosperity.

The West African goddess, **Mawu** is the creator of the earth and all things on it. She gives life, and can take it away. She is the mother of fate.

Mbaba Mwana Waresa is a fertility goddess of the Zulu region of Africa. She represents rain, and agriculture, and is credited with having invented beer. She is considered the link between heaven and earth.

The Buddhist goddess of compassion **Guan Yin** can manifest in practically any form to help the victims of natural disasters or of violence. She is also the one that childless women pray to for help.

Xi Wang-Mu is the Chinese goddess of immortality, and femininity. She has a palace of jade in the magical Kun-Lun mountains surrounded by a wall made of pure gold, one thousand miles long.

The Japanese sun goddess **Amaterasu** allows people to see their beauty and potential; she is considered the predecessor of the Japanese Imperial family.

The Japanese goddess **Konohana Sakuya** is the guardian of flowers and trees, and is said to preside over Mt. Fuji, preventing it from erupting.

Saraswati is the Hindu goddess of art, music, learning and wisdom. She protects all people interested in knowledge, especially students, teachers, and scientists.

The Hindu goddess of wealth, **Lakshmi** represents all forms of prosperity. The two elephants that accompany her represent hard work, and her image is used to indicate fortune.

The Tibetan goddess **Tara** has a dual personality, represented by the colors white and green. A white Tara is peaceful and compassionate, and brings long life and peace; while green Tara is determined and fierce in overcoming obstacles, and saves people from spiritual dangers.